For all refugees and those who help them
A.B.

For S.B.
S.U.

£5 from the sale of every book will go to War Child UK,
registered charity number: 1071659

The following organisations and individuals contributed to this book either by dramatically reducing profit
or making no profit at all: Anne Booth, Sam Usher, Nosy Crow, Imago, L.E.G.O. S.p.A., XY Digital,
The Bookseller magazine, GBS, LDA, Bounce Marketing and every British bookseller who has stocked this book.

First published 2015 by Nosy Crow Ltd
The Crow's Nest, 10a Lant Street
London SE1 1QR
www.nosycrow.com

ISBN 978 0 85763 741 3

Printed in Italy by Imago

Papers used by Nosy Crow are made from wood
grown in sustainable forests.

1 3 5 7 9 8 6 4 2

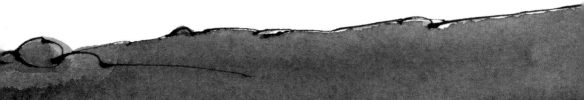

Refuge

Anne Booth & Sam Usher

The man led me, and I carried the woman all the way to Bethlehem . . .

And then the baby was born.

The shepherds came first . . .

And after them
came the kings . . .

When the last king left, the scent of frankincense lingering in the air, we all slept and the man had a dream.

A dream of danger.

He woke long before the sun rose and told
the woman. She took the baby, and kissed him.
She smelt his sweet baby breath, and felt his soft,
warm, baby skin and how his lashes tickled her
cheek, as he sleepily nuzzled her neck.

"Time to go," she said.

Then they wrapped him up warm and kissed him again, and the man came to get me. He patted me between the ears and led me out.

"Come on, old friend, we're off on a journey again."
And we left some gold for the innkeeper,
for he had been good to us, when others had not.

And we set off . . .

. . . under starlight, through empty streets,

whilst people were sleeping,
hoping for the kindness of strangers.

Again.

And we passed the shepherds in the fields,
and there were whispered blessings,

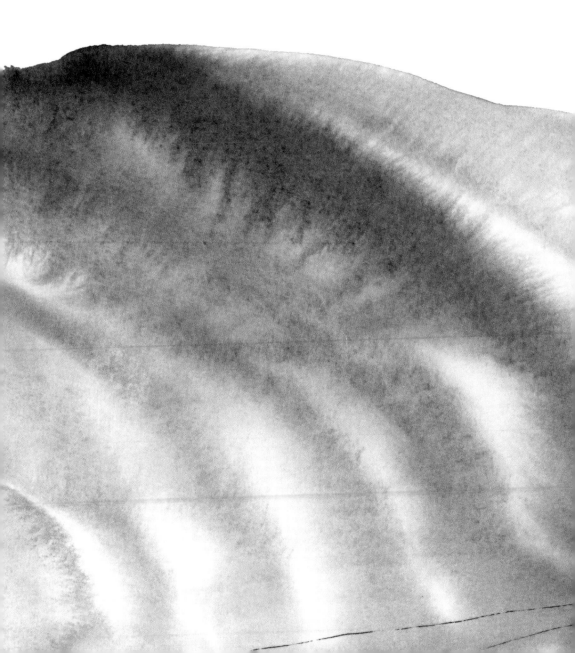

and the movement of sheep in the darkness,
and the clasp of rough hands,
and the love of warm hearts.

And I kept walking, carrying my precious load,
and the woman held the baby close to her heart,
and she and the man talked, about journeys,
and dreams and warnings,
and the love of a baby,
and the kindness of strangers.

And when we rested,
and they were frightened,
they took hope from each other,
and from the baby's tiny first smile.

And we entered into Egypt . . .

. . . and we found refuge.

Little Angels

Mal Peet

Illustrated by Ian Newsham

Oxford

Five little angels
in the Christmas play.
One pulled a funny face.